Meow!
Will you answer
the call for adventure?

Kitty

and the
Twilight Trouble

Greenwillow Books
An Imprint of HarperCollinsPublishers

For my mum and dad—P. H.

For Lizzie's little future reader!—J. L.

Kitty and the Twilight Trouble
Text copyright © 2021 by Paula Harrison. Illustrations copyright © 2021 by Jenny Løvlie.
First published in the United Kingdom in 2021 by Oxford University Press; first published in the United States by Greenwillow Books, 2021

www.harpercollinschildrens.com. The text of this book is set in Berling LT Std.

Library of Congress Control Number: 2021941385
ISBN 978-0-06-293583-0 (hardcover) — ISBN 978-0-06-293582-3 (paperback)
21 22 23 24 25 PC/LSCC 10 9 8 7 6 5 4 3 2 1
First Edition
Greenwillow Books

Contents

Meet Kitty & Her Cat Crew

Kitty

Kitty has special powers—but is she ready to be a superhero just like her mom?

Luckily, Kitty's cat crew has faith in her and shows Kitty the hero that lies within.

Pumpkin

A stray ginger kitten who is utterly devoted to Kitty.

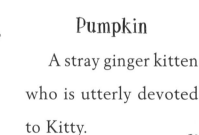

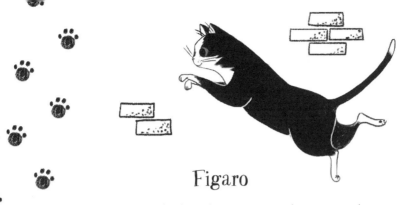

Figaro

Wise and kind, Figaro knows the neighborhood like the back of his paw.

Pixie

Pixie has a nose for trouble and whiskers for mischief!

Katsumi

Sleek and sophisticated, Katsumi is quick to call Kitty at the first sign of trouble.

Chapter 1

Kitty bounded across the school playground at dismissal time. "Guess what?" She grinned at Dad and her little brother, Max. "There's a carnival setting up at Taylor Park."

"Really? That sounds fun!" Dad

said, smiling.

"They open tomorrow!" Kitty said breathlessly. "And there will be rides and candy apples and everything! The whole class was talking about it today." Max's

2

eyes went big and round. "Ooh, candy apples!"

Kitty clasped her hands together. "Can we go? Please?"

"Maybe this weekend," Dad replied, steering them toward the schoolyard gate. "Let's see what your mom says."

Kitty skipped ahead, with thoughts of cotton candy and rides on the Ferris wheel going around in her head. She rushed through the gate into the park. Birds were singing in the treetops, and bright sunshine drifted through the branches. Kitty felt her superpowers bubbling inside her. She raced forward and turned three somersaults in a row, landing neatly on her feet.

Kitty had a special secret. She had

4

catlike superpowers, and that was why she could jump and somersault so easily. With her superpowered senses, she could see in the dark and hear sounds from miles away. Her favorite part of being a superhero in training was talking to animals. She loved going on adventures in the moonlight with her cat crew, skipping over the rooftops after dark.

Kitty leaped up to swing from a tree branch. Her dad and Max were quite a ways behind, and she knew she should wait for them. Suddenly, she glimpsed a furry white cat peeping out from behind a tree trunk. "Come out, Pixie! I know you're hiding over there." She grinned. Pixie was one of her cat crew. The little white cat was always full of mischief and loved to play tricks on everyone.

"MEOW! Got you, Kitty." Pixie jumped out and pounced on Kitty's foot.

"Hello, Pixie!" Kitty said, laughing. "What are you doing here?"

"I came to tell you my exciting news!" Pixie's green eyes sparkled. "I've made a new friend—a cat called Hazel—and she's amazing!"

Kitty smiled. "I don't think I've met any cats called Hazel."

"She showed me how to do lots of cool tricks. Just watch this!" Pixie dashed over

to the playground and leaped onto a swing, hanging upside down by her tail. Then she balanced by the tips of her paws on the seesaw.

"Amazing!" said Kitty admiringly.

Pixie leaped back down. "I told her

that you're a superhero, and I talked about the adventures we've had. She said she'd like to meet you. Can I bring her over tonight?"

"Of course you can!" said Kitty. "I'd love to meet your friend."

"Thanks, Kitty! See you soon." Pixie dashed away through the trees.

🐾 🐾 🐾

Kitty waited for Pixie on her window seat at bedtime. Her best friend, a ginger kitten called Pumpkin, sat snuggled up beside her. Kitty had met Pumpkin on her very first adventure as a superhero in training. Now he lived with them and slept on Kitty's bed every night.

The sky darkened and a bright

full moon rose above the buildings and houses. Cars with shining headlights zoomed along the street below. Kitty peered out of the window, expecting to see Pixie springing jauntily around the chimneys.

"Are you sure Pixie said she'd come tonight?" Pumpkin asked with a yawn.

"She definitely said tonight." Kitty frowned a little. "I wonder if she's changed her mind."

"I think we should just go to bed." Pumpkin snuggled against her arm. "I'm very sleepy!"

"Look, here she comes!"

Kitty spotted a cat in the distance. Then she looked more closely with her special night vision.

"No, wait! That's Figaro."

Figaro leaped across the rooftops, his white paws flashing in the moonlight. He

13

jumped down to Kitty's windowsill and smoothed his whiskers. "Good evening, Kitty. I'm afraid I have some bad news. I thought it would be best if you heard it straight from me."

"What happened?" said Kitty in alarm. "Does someone need my help?"

Figaro groomed his sleek black fur before replying. "No, it's about Pixie. She told me she was supposed to see you this evening, but she's visiting with another cat instead."

"Oh! That must be Hazel—her new

friend," said Kitty.
Figaro nodded
seriously. "They left saying
they wanted to have an
adventure of their own. Hazel
also said she was far too busy
to meet some silly human."

"That's not very nice!" said Pumpkin indignantly.

Kitty's heart sank. She'd been looking forward to meeting Pixie's new friend. "Maybe she didn't really mean it."

"But there's even more!" Figaro's eyes flashed, and he paused, checking to see that he had their attention. "Hazel said that *she* was a cat superhero with all kinds of special powers, and that's why they're having their own adventure. She told me she had

16

important superhero work to do!"

Kitty looked at Figaro with surprise. She hadn't heard of a cat having superpowers before. "That's amazing! I wonder where they've gone."

"They didn't tell me." Figaro sat back and rubbed his ear with one paw. "I don't like that Hazel, though. All of us used to be a team before she came along."

"She might be really nice once you get to know her," Kitty managed to say.

Figaro sniffed and began grooming his sleek black-and-white tail.

Kitty gazed out into the darkness. A sprinkling of stars sparkled in the velvet-black sky, but thick clouds had hidden the moon.

Kitty didn't want to say bad things about a cat she hadn't even met, but in her heart she agreed with Figaro. She loved her cat crew. They had been on so many great adventures together. She hoped this new cat, Hazel, wasn't going to come along and spoil it all.

19

Chapter 2

The following evening, the moon smiled down on the city like a wise old face. Kitty waited at her bedroom window again, listening to every tiny sound with her superpowered hearing. Cars roared up and down the street, and an owl hooted somewhere inside the park.

Kitty's mom and dad had told her they'd take her to the carnival the following day. As she sat by the window, she imagined the lights and music of the merry-go-round and the smell of the hot dogs. She couldn't wait to go and try out some of the rides!

The moon climbed slowly above the trees and the houses. Kitty watched carefully, but there was still no sign of Pixie. She sighed, and Pumpkin stirred on her lap, his whiskers twitching as he dreamed.

Kitty turned away from the window, wondering why Pixie didn't want to visit her anymore. She was about to lift Pumpkin into her arms and close the curtain, when she spotted two cats skipping over a distant rooftop. One of them was Pixie, her fluffy white coat gleaming in the moonlight. The other was a brown-and-white tabby with a long, sleek tail.

Kitty carefully laid the sleeping Pumpkin on her bed. Then she climbed out of her window and leaped lightly onto the roof. The stars winked in the darkness, and a gentle breeze swirled around her. "Pixie!" she called. "I'm over here."

Pixie and her friend kept on playing. They were leaping over a chimney and giggling.

Kitty hurried across the rooftops toward them. The other cat must be Hazel, she thought. "Pixie," she called. "I waited for you last night."

The tabby cat whispered something

in Pixie's ear and laughed.

Pixie turned around and skipped over to Kitty. "Hi, Kitty, this is Hazel." She waved her paw toward the tabby cat.

"Hello, Hazel." Kitty smiled at the tabby, who looked back warily. She noticed that the cats had matching red bandannas tied around their throats. Each one had the letter H sewn on to it.

"Sorry I didn't come to see you yesterday," said Pixie. "We were really busy having an adventure."

"That sounds like fun!" replied Kitty. "Wow, I love your matching scarves. They look so pretty."

"Oh, thanks!" Pixie flicked her tail proudly. "We're wearing them because . . ."

"Shh, don't tell the

human!" Hazel gave Pixie a nudge. Then she dashed away across the rooftops. "Come on, Pixie. I know a great place we can explore."

Kitty flushed. She was trying to be nice, but Hazel didn't seem very interested in being friends.

Pixie didn't notice Hazel's rudeness. The little white cat raced after her new friend, calling back, "Got to go, Kitty! See you tomorrow, maybe."

Kitty watched them run away over the rooftops. Then she walked slowly back home and climbed through her bedroom window.

"What happened? Is someone in trouble?" Pumpkin asked sleepily.

"Everything's fine, don't worry." Kitty snuggled down in bed and turned out the light.

Pumpkin went back to sleep, but Kitty gazed at the moon peeping through the curtains. Why had Hazel been so rude, when she was only trying to be friends? Kitty tried to remember whether she'd said something wrong, but she didn't think she had.

She turned over in bed. She wished Pixie had stopped to talk rather than run off for an adventure. After all, they had been friends long before Hazel came along.

After dinner the next day, Kitty's mom and dad took Kitty and Max to the carnival. They walked toward Taylor Park as the sun set and streaks of orange hung in the sky like bright streamers.

Kitty thought about Pixie and Hazel for a moment. She wondered whether they had gone for another adventure by themselves.

"You're very quiet, Kitty," said Mom. "Are you looking forward to the rides?"

"Yes, I can't wait!" Kitty's heart skipped as she heard the carnival music in the distance. People crowded into the narrow street leading to Taylor Park, and Kitty spotted the Ferris wheel with its flashing rainbow lights. The music grew louder and the smell of popcorn and cotton

33

candy drifted through the evening air.

Pumpkin and Figaro had come to see what the carnival was all about.

Pumpkin gazed around with wide eyes. "It's very noisy, isn't it?" he said, a little doubtfully.

"Yes, but there is so much to do!" Figaro leaped onto the hook-a-duck game and swiped playfully at the plastic ducks with his paw.

After a moment, Pumpkin leaped up beside him and the two cats swiped

at the toy ducks together. Kitty watched
them wistfully. It looked like a fun game
for a cat.

Max asked Kitty to take him
on the alligator bounce

ride. When she returned, she found Figaro and Pumpkin by the candy apple stand. Figaro was frowning deeply.

"What's wrong?" asked Kitty.

"It's that Hazel again!" snapped Figaro. "She and Pixie are rushing around looking for someone to rescue. It's as if Pixie has forgotten that she was a part of *our* cat crew first!"

"Oh!" Kitty sighed. Maybe Pixie thought Hazel was a better superhero than her.

"I honestly don't know why she's hanging around with Hazel," Figaro went on. "We had *millions* of adventures together before that tabby cat came along."

Kitty took a deep breath. "But it's nice that they want to help! If you've

got superpowers then you should use them to make the world a better place."

Pumpkin rubbed against her legs. "There aren't any superheroes as good as you, though."

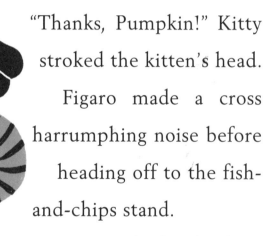

"Thanks, Pumpkin!" Kitty stroked the kitten's head. Figaro made a cross harrumphing noise before heading off to the fish-and-chips stand.

Kitty sighed. Thinking about Pixie and Hazel was

starting to make her head ache. "Come on!" she said to Pumpkin. "There's a milk-bottle toss game over here. Should I try it? Maybe I can win a prize." She handed the game operator some coins and he gave her three balls.

While she waited for her turn, Kitty noticed Pixie and Hazel climbing up the side of the cotton candy stall. They jumped around, chasing each other's tails, their matching red scarves flapping.

Pixie hung upside down from the stall and swiped some cotton candy from a small boy. She stuck her paw in her mouth and licked off the sugary pink mixture.

The little boy noticed his food was gone and began to cry. Hazel giggled.

Kitty frowned. That wasn't superhero behavior at all.

"Kitty, it's your turn!" said Pumpkin, and Kitty turned back to the milk-bottle throw.

She knocked down two of the heavy bottles and chose a rainbow-colored bouncy ball as her prize. Her mom and dad and Max arrived and they all took turns at knocking milk bottles down. By the time Kitty looked back at the cotton candy stall, Pixie and Hazel had disappeared.

"Kitty, I need your help!" Figaro came rushing back, his whiskers twitching in panic. "There's a whole nest of baby birds in terrible danger. Hurry!"

Kitty and Pumpkin followed Figaro through the crowd. Figaro stopped beside the rollercoaster and clutched his cheek. "Oh dear, this is terrible! I can't look!"

The rollercoaster went

past in a whirl of speed and noise, and the riders shouted out in excitement. Kitty followed Figaro's gaze. An old oak tree stood beside the rollercoaster, with one branch stretching out toward the ride.

Kitty spotted the birds' nest right away. It was perched in the crook of a branch beside the rollercoaster, and every time the ride zoomed past, the nest trembled a little closer to the edge. Three little feathery heads peeped over the side of the nest. The birds' eyes were wide with fright, and their tiny wings flapped helplessly.

Pumpkin gasped. "The poor things! Do something, Kitty!"

Kitty dashed into the shadows. She pulled off her coat and put on her black cape and mask. Then she leaped into the air, grabbed the lowest branch of the tree,

and swung herself up. Quickly,
she began to climb. She had to
reach the little birds before it
was too late!

Chapter 3

The moonlight poured down, and Kitty felt her superpowers tingling inside her. She climbed swiftly, swinging from one branch to the next, hidden in the shadows. Then she shinned up the tree trunk, digging her sneakers into the rough bark to find a foothold.

The birds' beaks were open as if they were calling for help, but their cheeping was almost drowned out by the carnival music and the whoosh of the rollercoaster. Kitty used her super hearing to zoom in on their tiny cries.

"It's all right—I'm coming to rescue you!" Kitty called, hoping they could hear her.

47

The ride zoomed past, making the tree shake furiously. The flashing lights dazed Kitty, and the screeching machinery made her head ache. But she clung on, holding tight to the branch with her fingertips.

The birds nest wobbled dangerously as the rollercoaster passed by. Kitty watched in horror as the nest tipped sideways and a tiny feathery shape dangled over the edge. She climbed faster, her heart racing. She had to reach the nest before the ride circled around again and sent the little birds crashing to the ground.

Suddenly, two cats came climbing up the side of the rollercoaster frame. Hazel and Pixie clambered along the metal beams, heading for the tree. Hazel leaped from the rollercoaster onto Kitty's branch, knocking her off balance.

Kitty steadied herself as the branch wobbled. "Hey, what's going on?" she asked, but Hazel ignored her.

Pixie leaped from the rollercoaster to the branch and followed Hazel up the tree. "Hi, Kitty. I can't stop," she mewed. "We're rescuing creatures in peril!"

"Pixie—wait!" called Kitty, but Pixie had already dashed away to join her friend.

Hazel grabbed the birds' nest, making it tip even farther. One of the little birds slipped out, its stubby wings fluttering in panic. Luckily, Pixie caught the bird and put it back into the nest again.

"Stop that silly cheeping!" Hazel told the birds rudely. "I am a cat superhero, and I know exactly what I'm doing." She grabbed the side of the nest with her mouth and began making her way down the tree.

Kitty also began to climb again, her eyes fixed on the little birds. When

Hazel made an extra big jump and lost her grip on the nest, Kitty swung down quickly to catch it and the baby birds just in the nick of time. The birds' parents, who had just arrived, flew around her in a panic.

"It's all right!" Kitty told them. "Your babies are much safer away from that rollercoaster." She turned to find the next foothold, but Hazel snatched the nest back without even saying thank you.

Kitty followed the two cats, sighing with relief when they reached the bottom without dropping the birds. "You have to be more careful!" she said, as Hazel dumped the nest on the ground. "These little birds were in terrible danger. . . ."

"*You* shouldn't get in the way!" interrupted Hazel. "You could have ruined the whole mission. *I* had everything under control because *I* am a real cat superhero, not just a silly human pretending to be a cat."

"That's not fair at all!" cried Kitty.

Hazel twitched her whiskers and gave Kitty a cold stare. "Pixie is *my* sidekick now. She doesn't need *you* anymore! You should leave the superhero stuff to us from now on."

Pixie glanced sideways at Kitty before turning away quickly.

Kitty felt tears prick her eyes. She hadn't expected Hazel to be so mean. Why hadn't Pixie stuck up for her? She thought they were friends.

"Anyway, we can't hang around here chatting with you," Hazel went on. "We have important rescue work to do. Come on, Pixie!" She marched off, ignoring the cheeping birds in their nest on the ground.

Pixie slunk after her.

Kitty kneeled down and took the birds' nest carefully in her hands.

"Kitty, what happened?" Figaro came running up with Pumpkin beside him. "We saw Hazel and Pixie at the top of the tree."

"I think they wanted to be the ones

56

to save the day," said Kitty. "Or maybe they didn't believe I'd be able to rescue the birds by myself."

Figaro shook his head. "That Hazel is a menace! I don't know why Pixie thinks she's so wonderful. I didn't see her use any superpowers at all!"

Kitty looked down at the three little birds huddled together in the nest. Their parents were fussing over them worriedly. The baby birds stared back at Kitty with wide eyes. Keeping them safe was what mattered now. "Let's find a better place to put your nest," she said. "I think you need a nice place to sleep."

The largest fledgling piped up in a tiny voice. "I'm too excited to sleep. That was my very first adventure, and I think it was amazing!"

Kitty smiled and stroked his downy head. "I'm just glad you're okay. Should we find a new home for you?"

"How about that hawthorn bush?

I'm sure it'll be nice and quiet in there." Pumpkin nodded to a patch of brambles, away from the bright lights and the noise of the rides.

"Oh, yes please!" said the baby birds' father. "That would be a wonderful place for our nest."

Kitty used her gymnastic skills to find a way through the tightly woven branches. Her night vision let her see easily in the dark undergrowth.

Searching carefully, she found a sturdy branch in the middle that was perfect for the little nest. The birds' parents fluttered above the hawthorn bush, thanking her for her help.

Kitty checked that the nest was balanced safely on the branch. She couldn't help thinking about what Hazel had said to her:

I am a real cat superhero, not just a silly human pretending to be a cat. That wasn't fair at all. She wasn't pretending to be anything.

She swallowed, wondering

whether Pixie or Figaro had ever thought she was pretending to be a cat, too.

"Can I come on another adventure with you?" asked the largest fledgling. "Please? It was so much fun!"

"I don't think that's a good idea," Kitty replied. "You're still a bit young to be having adventures." She turned away, still thinking about Hazel and Pixie.

The baby bird gave a disappointed cheep before huddling down inside the nest with his brother and sister. Kitty slipped through the tangle of branches and headed back toward the flashing lights of the carnival. She met Figaro and Pumpkin, and they spotted Kitty's family at the candy apple stand.

"Is everything all right, Kitty?" asked Pumpkin.

"I was thinking about

Pixie and how excited she is to have made friends with Hazel." Kitty sighed. She missed the little white cat terribly, but Pixie hadn't even stuck up for her when Hazel had said mean things.

Kitty was silent most of the way home. Her feet felt heavy, and her head was pounding after the loud carnival music.

"Is something wrong?" her mom asked her quietly. "You haven't said anything since we left the fair."

"No, not really," said Kitty. "It's just . . . I thought everyone would understand that I'm just trying to help people with my superpowers."

Her mom put an arm around her. "Being a superhero isn't always easy. Sometimes other people won't understand what you're trying to do, but that doesn't mean you should give up. There are people and animals out there who will need your help. Remember—you're stronger than you think!"

"Thanks, Mom." Kitty gave her a hug. Her heart felt a little lighter as they headed home in the moonlight.

She knew she had tried to
help the birds the best she
could.

67

Chapter 4

That night, Kitty dreamed that she was stuck on the merry-go-round at the carnival. Pixie was there, too, eating cotton candy and giggling with Hazel. The merry-go-round spun faster and faster and made her dizzy. Then she heard Figaro shouting her name and his voice grew louder and louder and louder.

Kitty sat up straight in bed. The wind whispered at the open window, making the curtains sway. She rubbed her eyes sleepily. She could still hear Figaro calling her. That part wasn't a dream at all!

She slipped out of bed, careful not to disturb Pumpkin, who was asleep on her pillow. Running to the window, she peered out into the darkness.

"Kitty, I'm so glad to see you!" cried

Figaro,

dashing toward her.

"What's the matter?" Kitty

climbed over the windowsill and joined

him on the roof. The moon shined brightly,

pouring silver light over all the houses.

"It's Pixie and Hazel!" puffed

Figaro, trying to catch

his breath.

Kitty's eyes widened in alarm. Figaro always liked to be dignified and grand. She'd never seen him rush around like this before. His black-and-white fur was standing on end, and his whiskers were shaking.

"They've gone too far this time . . . they're in terrible danger!" he went on. "We must leave for the carnival *immediately*."

Kitty dashed inside and put on her superhero outfit. If Pixie was in trouble Kitty would be there to help, no matter what had happened earlier that evening. Tying her black cape around her neck, she jumped back out of the window. Her superpowers tingled inside her like electricity, and her heartbeat quickened.

Pumpkin had woken up and he followed her to the window. "What's happening?" he asked.

"Pixie's in trouble! We have to

hurry." Kitty gathered Pumpkin into her arms and dashed after Figaro.

The city streets below were quiet. Only the occasional hoot of an owl or the rustle of a mouse broke the silence. Kitty and Figaro raced across the rooftops. They climbed drainpipes, jumped over chimneys, and swung around satellite dishes. At last, Kitty spotted the park in the distance.

Figaro leaped onto the pavement and ran down the street that led to the carnival. The rides were still and silent, and the food stands were empty. The only thing moving was an empty bag blowing across the grass.

Kitty shivered. The carnival looked spooky in the dark. Then she took a deep breath. She was here to help Pixie and Hazel, she reminded herself. There was no time to be scared!

Figaro stopped at the bottom of the Ferris wheel. "I told them not to go up there!" he cried. "If only they had listened to me."

Kitty gazed at the huge wheel

75

with its round frame and metal spokes. The moon had risen behind the ride, and the shiny metal frame glinted in the pale light. Kitty spotted two tiny shapes right at the top of the wheel. Hazel was hanging from the frame by the tips of her paws. Pixie was dangling from Hazel's tail.

Kitty gulped. The ride's metal frame was made from narrow beams. They looked slippery and hard to climb. No wonder Pixie and Hazel were in such terrible trouble.

"Pixie said they'd seen a creature in danger," Figaro told Kitty. "And that's why they decided to go up there."

Pumpkin gasped. "But it's such a long way to fall!"

Kitty used her special night vision to

zoom in on the frightened cats at the top of the ride. She suddenly wondered whether Hazel's tales of superpowers had been true, but there was no time to think about that now. "Don't worry!" she told Pumpkin. "I can reach them."

"Be careful, Kitty!" cried Figaro.

Kitty began climbing the frame of the ride, using the narrow metal beams.

"We're up here, Kitty. Please help us!" Pixie wailed from high above.

Kitty's heart raced and she climbed

even faster. Rain began to fall, making the thin metal beams even more slippery. Kitty gripped them tightly as she swung from one bar to the next. She edged along the narrow spokes, spreading her arms wide to keep her balance.

When she glanced at the ground, her heart skipped a beat. It really was a long way down. *You can do this,* she told herself. *You're a superhero in training!*

The wind grew stronger, blowing raindrops into Kitty's face. Water dripped from her black cape, but she went on climbing bravely. She was determined to reach the cats, no matter how difficult it was.

"Hurry, Kitty!" squeaked Pixie. "I don't think I can hold on for much longer."

Kitty looked up in alarm. Pixie had slipped down Hazel's tail and was holding on with one paw. Pumpkin and Figaro's scared faces gazed up at them from the ground far below.

"Hold on! I'm almost there." Kitty jumped onto one of the wheel's cars and continued her climbing.

At last she reached the top of the ride. Balancing on the highest beam, she pulled Hazel up with both hands. Hazel's fur stood on end and her paws trembled as Kitty set her safely down on the beam.

Just as Kitty was about to scoop Pixie up, a windy blast of rain pelted them all. Pixie let out a terrible screech, losing her grip on Hazel's tail and tumbling downward. Quick as a whisker, Kitty hooked her feet over the metal bar and swung through the air like an acrobat.

83

The stormy breeze whooshed past her. She grabbed hold of Pixie's paws and held the cat tightly as they swung together. Then she dropped Pixie neatly inside one of the cars. As she swung back to the beam, she nearly lost her balance. For a terrible moment, she stared at the ground far below. Then she grabbed the beam with one hand and pulled herself to safety.

Hazel stared at her, open-mouthed, her whiskers shaking.

Kitty tried to catch her breath, but her heart was racing. "Are you all right?" she asked Hazel.

"*Yowl!*" cried Hazel, tears rolling down her cheeks.

Kitty lifted Hazel carefully with one arm and climbed down to the car where she'd left Pixie. The two cats huddled together on the seats, while Kitty perched on the bars in front.

"Thank you for helping us, Kitty!"

Pixie shivered. "I didn't realize the ride was so tall. I was climbing perfectly until I lost my balance for a moment . . ."

Kitty frowned. "But you could have been seriously hurt! What on earth were you doing climbing all the way up here?"

Chapter 5

Hazel and Pixie sat hunched in the car at the top of the Ferris wheel. Hazel's whiskers were still shaking.

"You're safe now," Kitty said gently. "But tell me why you came up here. Figaro said there was an animal in danger."

"We saw a baby bird stuck at the top and we climbed up to save him . . . ," Hazel mumbled. "But then we slipped and got into trouble."

"Where did you see the bird?" asked Kitty, alarmed.

"On one of those cars." Pixie pointed upward. "But I can't see him anymore."

Kitty peered at the cars hanging overhead. The wind blew strongly, making them rock. "Wait for me here!" she told the cats. Then she sprang for the nearest beam and ran along the frame of the ride. She searched the first car but found nothing. Climbing to the next one, she heard a tiny chirping sound.

"Hello," she called. "My name's Kitty. Are you all right?"

"Oh, dear!" cheeped a small voice. "How will I ever get down?"

"I'll help you! Please don't worry." Kitty hunted all around and found the baby bird clinging to the back of the car. His feathers were ruffled, and his eyes were wide with fright. Kitty scooped him up and settled him on her shoulder.

"Oh, thank you!" he squeaked, clinging to her with his stubby wings.

"That's all right!" Kitty looked more closely. She was sure she recognized the little bird. "Aren't you one of the birds from the nest beside the rollercoaster? Why are you all the way up here?"

The bird snuggled against Kitty's neck. "I just wanted to prove that I'm old enough to have an adventure. I thought it would be exciting, but it's horrible and scary and I want to go home!"

"But how did you get here?" asked Kitty. "It's a very long way from your nest."

"I hid in one of

the cars when no one was looking," the baby bird said. "Then the ride stopped, and everyone went home. That's when I knew I was stuck because I haven't learned how to fly yet. I tried to hop back down but I just couldn't!"

Kitty's heart sank. She remembered that the little bird had wanted an adventure, and she had said he was too young. If she had taken more time to talk to him, he might never have put himself in danger. She had been upset after Hazel called her *a silly human*, and that had pushed everything else out of her head.

"I know I said you were too young for adventures, but that was unfair of me," she told the baby bird. "Once you've learned to fly, we can go on an adventure together. Would you like that?"

"Yes, please! I'd love that," the bird said eagerly.

"Then I promise you that's what we'll do!" Kitty smiled at the bird, and he flapped his wings happily.

Kitty made sure he was perched safely on her shoulder before climbing back to Pixie and Hazel. The wind blew in strong gusts, making the Ferris wheel cars rock back and forth.

"We'd better climb down quickly," Kitty told the cats. "It's not safe to stay up here in such a strong wind."

"I can't!" Hazel's voice wobbled. "I'm worried that I'll slip again."

"I'll help you. Climb onto my arm." Kitty helped the tabby cat settle on her other shoulder. Then, guiding Pixie

gently, she made her way down the big
wheel.

The rain stopped and the stars
appeared again, twinkling like diamonds
in the dark sky. Kitty clambered down

slowly, careful not to slip on the wet beams. At last she leaped gracefully from the Ferris wheel to the ground.

"Hooray, you're all safe!" Pumpkin jumped around and waved his stripy tail.

"Thank goodness!" Figaro said with relief in his voice. "I was afraid that something truly terrible would happen. All the time you were up there, I could hardly look!"

Kitty had expected Pixie to start chattering about everything they'd done, but instead the little white cat burst into tears. "I'm really sorry, Kitty," she sobbed. "I didn't mean to cause so much trouble. I thought Hazel was a superhero in training, just like you, and that everything would be all right!"

Figaro shook his head. "I *knew* the superhero thing couldn't be real."

Hazel stared down at her paws. "I just liked pretending," she muttered. "And I really *was* worried about the baby bird."

"You shouldn't have done it!" snapped Figaro. "I had to run all the way to Kitty's house when you got yourselves stuck. I nearly scraped my paw on a chimney."

"It's all right, Figaro." Kitty calmed him down.

Tears were dripping down Pixie's cheeks. Hazel stared at the ground, her tail drooping.

"I think you made some mistakes," said Kitty. "But you were also very brave. Not many cats would have had the courage to climb all the way up the Ferris wheel."

Pixie sniffed and wiped her cheek with her paw.

Kitty tried to think of what her mom would say. "I know you wanted to be like superheroes. But I think being a

superhero is about more than being brave. It's about being kind, too, and looking for the best in others—animals and humans." She smiled at the baby bird still perched on her shoulder. "You can't help others if you can't be kind."

Hazel nodded. "I'm sorry, Kitty. I shouldn't have been so unfair to you. Do you think . . . um . . . that we could be friends?"

"Of course we can!" Kitty smiled.

"I'm sorry, too!" Pixie perked up a little. "I missed being part of the cat

crew and meeting up at your house, Kitty. Do you think all of us could go back there now together?"

"I think that's the best idea in the world!" said Kitty.

Chapter 6

Kitty took the baby bird back to his nest in the bushes. The birds' parents had returned after hunting for grubs. They thanked Kitty for looking after their baby again, and snuggled down together for the night.

Pixie led the way out of the dark carnival. Kitty walked alongside Hazel, who cast shy glances up at her. They climbed the drainpipe at the end of the alley and scampered along the rooftops back to Kitty's house. Hazel followed Kitty, trying to copy the way she jumped and ran.

The clouds drifted away and the moon shined even brighter than before. The roofs glistened with thousands of raindrops, and each puddle on the pavement reflected a tiny pale moon.

Kitty smiled widely as they reached the flat roof above her bedroom. She was so happy to have her friends all together again. She somersaulted over the chimney, her long cape flying out around her.

Figaro's stomach rumbled loudly. "Perhaps it's time for a midnight snack! Do you have any food inside, Kitty?"

"My dad bought some fresh mackerel from the fish store today," Kitty told him. "I'll bring everything outside and we can have a proper midnight feast."

"I'll help you, Kitty!" meowed Pumpkin.

Kitty and Pumpkin climbed inside and gathered everything into a picnic basket. There were orange plates and bowls, and a picnic blanket covered in a paw-print pattern. Kitty added some homemade chocolate chip cookies to the basket and a bottle of lemonade.

Returning to the rooftop, she found Hazel listening to Figaro as he explained how important it was to groom her tail and whiskers correctly.

"Always start at the root of your fur and then groom outward with one smooth movement!" he said, demonstrating with a grand flourish.

Pixie bounced up and down when she saw the picnic basket. "Ooh, thanks Kitty! Let me help you with the blanket."

They laid the blanket on the flat rooftop, and Kitty handed out the pieces of mackerel. Pixie also took a cookie, as she loved anything with chocolate.

Hazel took a nibble of her fish. Then she gave a shy cough. "Um . . . Kitty? It must be amazing to be a superhero. I've

never seen anyone climb and balance like you can. I would love to be just like you!"

"Kitty is the best!" said Pumpkin. "We've had so many adventures together."

Hazel twitched her whiskers eagerly. "I'd like to hear about them. If you don't mind, that is!"

"All right! Let me think . . ." Kitty brushed the cookie crumbs from her hands. "I know! There was once a precious golden tiger statue that was stolen from the museum. Its eyes were made of real emeralds, and it had a special secret . . ."

Hazel's eyes grew wider as Kitty told her all about the thief who stole the tiger statue, and how she got it back. Figaro added a few details to the story here and there.

The moon smiled down at the rooftop and the stars twinkled. Kitty looked at the eager faces of the cats and she felt a warm glow spread inside her. It was wonderful to jump and climb and turn somersaults, but having good friends was really special, too.

Super Facts About Cats

Super Speed

Have you ever seen a cat make a quick escape from a dog? If so, you know they can move *really* fast—up to thirty miles per hour!

Super Hearing

Cats have an incredible sense of hearing and can swivel their ears to pinpoint even the tiniest of sounds.

Super Reflexes

Have you ever heard the saying, "Cats always land on their feet"? People say this because cats have amazing reflexes. If a cat

is falling, it can quickly sense how
to move its body into the right position
to land safely.

Super Vision

Cats have amazing nighttime vision. Their
incredible ability to see in low light allows
them to hunt for prey when it's dark outside.

Super Smell

Cats have a very powerful sense of smell.
Did you know that the pattern of ridges on
each cat's nose is as unique as a human's
fingerprints?

The Kitty books—
read them all!

Kitty's family has a secret. Her mom is a hero with catlike superpowers, and Kitty knows that one day she'll have special powers and the chance to use them, too. That day comes sooner than expected, when a friendly black cat named Figaro comes to Kitty's bedroom window to ask for help. But the world at night is a scary place— is Kitty brave enough to step out into the darkness for a thrilling moonlight adventure?

Girl by day. Cat by night. Ready for adventure.

Written by **Paula Harrison** · Illustrated by **Jenny Løvlie**

Kitty can't wait to see the priceless Golden Tiger Statue with her own eyes. Legend says that if you hold the statue, you can make your greatest wish come true. Kitty and her cat, Pumpkin, decide to sneak into the museum to see the statue at night, when no one else is around. But disaster strikes when the statue is stolen right in front of them! Can Kitty find the thief and return the precious statue before sunrise?

Kitty, Pumpkin, and Pixie discover a sky garden hidden high on a rooftop. It's a magical place, filled with beautiful flowers and sparkling fairy lights. Pixie is so excited, she wants to tell everyone about it—but the more cats discover the sky garden, the wilder it becomes! Soon the rooftop is overrun with unwelcome visitors. Can Kitty and her friends protect this secret, special place—and all the magical things growing in it—before it's too late?

When a new family moves into town, Kitty is excited to make another friend. But Ozzy, Kitty's new neighbor, is quiet and seems to have nothing in common with Kitty. When night approaches, Katsumi, a member of Kitty's cat crew, tells Kitty about a dog causing a commotion in the bakery. Kitty decides to use her catlike superpowers to investigate, and it turns out that Ozzy has his own superpowers, too! Together, they set off to track down the mischievous dog before he can cause even more damage.

Kitty can't w.
celebrate the Fes
Light in her towr
made a lantern tha
exactly like a ca
when the parade

Kitty spies a thief in the crowd. The
even steals the golden crown—the prize
best lantern. Can Kitty catch the thief,
the stolen belongings, and save the festi
without the help of her cat crew?